The Terrible Trainer

Other titles in the same series

Ghost Goalie

The Tigers football team are full of confidence about the next match. But their coach falls ill just before they are due to play! The Tigers are desperate. How can they win without him? Perhaps they can, with a very special bit of ghostly help . . .

Save the Pitch

It's the crucial last game of the season and the Tigers football team must win to go to the top of the League. But the pitch has been invaded by workmen laying new pipes, and it looks like the game will be called off. Can the Tigers get help – fast?

The Cup Final

The Tigers football team have to win this last game to win the Cup! But disaster strikes when their coach's head becomes stuck in some iron railings when trying to get the ball. What can they do to save the match?

Tigers on Television

The Tigers football team have a nail-biting match to play, and a local TV crew has come to film them in action. But the TV cameras have a terrible effect on the team's ghost trainer and he can't coach them properly! What can the Tigers do?

Ghost Striker

The Tigers football team are facing a difficult away match against a tough team, but they have got the special help of their ghost goalie . . . or have they? Things look bad when an old opponent arrives – intent on revenge!

The Terrible Trainer

J. BURCHETT AND S. VOGLER

ILLUSTRATED BY Guy Parker-Rees

BLOOMSBURY

LONDON BERLIN NEW YORK

For Laura and Matthew Neal

Bloomsbury Publishing, London, Berlin and New York

First published in Great Britain in 1998 by Bloomsbury Publishing Plc
36 Soho Square, London, W1D 3QY
This edition published in July 2010

Text copyright © Janet Burchett and Sara Vogler 1998
Illustrations copyright © Guy Parker-Rees 1998
The moral rights of the author and illustrator have been asserted

All rights reserved
No part of this publication may be reproduced or
transmitted by any means, electronic, mechanical, photocopying
or otherwise, without the prior permission of the publisher

A CIP catalogue record of this book is available from the British Library

ISBN 978 1 4088 0829 0

FSC
Mixed Sources
Product group from well-managed
forests and other controlled sources
Cert no. SGS-COC-2061
www.fsc.org
© 1996 Forest Stewardship Council

Printed in Great Britain by Clays Ltd, St Ives plc, Bungay, Suffolk

1 3 5 7 9 10 8 6 4 2

www.bloomsbury.com/childrens

THE TIGERS

Mona (GK)

Terry RICK Lisa Blocker

Joe ROB Ellen Kim

Bullseye Billy Bright

Logo Coach Mr. Bright

The Terrible Trainer

Billy Bright and the Tigers
Under-Tens Football Team
were in Tottingham Town Park.
They should have been
practising but they weren't.
They were writing their names

on a huge get-well card. It was for their coach, Billy's dad.

'What did your dad say about the match tomorrow?' asked Mona the goalkeeper.

'He didn't say anything,' said Billy. 'He can't talk. His throat's too sore.'

'He's only had his tonsils out,' said Blocker. 'I didn't stop talking when I had mine out.'

'Nothing could stop you talking!' laughed Ellen.

'But what about the match tomorrow?' said Mona. 'Will he be back by then?'

The Tigers were a good side, but they got into a muddle without their coach.

'No, he won't,' said Billy.

'He wrote me a note. It said he's found us another coach. He's called Mr Bawl.'

Everyone laughed.

'He must have been joking,' said Joe.

'What's his brother's name?' chuckled Terry. 'Mr Goalpost?'

'Your dad was probably dreaming,' said Blocker. 'I had funny dreams when I had my tonsils out.'

'You always have funny dreams, Blocker,' said Ellen.

'Billy'll coach us, won't you, Billy?' said Rob.

'You're a good coach,' said Lisa, 'when you get going.'

Whenever Billy's dad couldn't coach, Billy took over. He pretended he used a coaching book. Nobody knew the truth. Billy was really a hopeless coach. But he had help from Springer Spannell. Springer had once been Tottingham Town's most famous goalkeeper. He'd saved a vital penalty in the FA Cup final and Tottingham Town FC had won the Cup. Everyone had heard of Springer Spannell. But only Billy could see and hear him. Springer Spannell was . . . a ghost. Billy wasn't allowed to tell anyone

his secret. It was in Springer's
PhIFA rulebook.

Billy looked round the park. There was someone striding towards them in the distance. He was wearing football gear.

'It's Springer,' thought Billy.

'What's first, Coach?' asked Rick.

Billy wished Springer would hurry up.

'Let's see,' he said, trying to look clever. 'Sit downs.'

The team sat down on the pitch.

'Is that it?' asked Rob.

The Tigers started giggling.

'I meant sit ups,' laughed Billy.

'Call that training?' boomed a voice.

Billy spun round. There, in

front of him, was a man in
football kit. He had a whistle
round his neck and a football
under his arm. He was small
and skinny and he had a big
moustache. It wasn't Springer!

'What are you lolling about
for?' the man shouted. 'Call
yourselves Tigers? You're more

like my granny's tortoise. Now, where's Billy Bright?'

Billy put his hand up.

'I'm Mr Bawl,' yelled the man. 'I'm your trainer for the next three weeks. Right, you horrible specimens, fifty press-ups, up down, up down!'

The Tigers were gobsmacked. Surely nice Mr Bright hadn't sent them this coach.

'What are you waiting for?' boomed Mr Bawl. 'If you don't train, you don't play!'

'We don't know how to do press-ups,' said Lisa.

'We're only nine,' said Billy.

'I don't care if you're ninety,' snarled Mr Bawl. 'Fifty press-ups now or I'll double it!'

The Tigers lay on their tummies and tried to push themselves up with their arms. It was hard. It was even harder the second time. By the time they got to five they thought they'd explode. Mr Bawl strode up and down like a sergeant major on parade.

'SIX . . . Put some effort into

it,' he bawled. 'SEVEN . . . I've seen better press-ups from my sister's pet jellyfish. EIGHT . . . get those biceps bulging . . . NINE . . .'

Billy lifted his head for press-up number ten. There was a man on the touchline. The man was wobbly round the edges. Billy could see right through

him. It was like looking
through a mango jelly.

It was Springer Spannell.
   'Sorry I'm late, Billy,' he
called. 'The bus broke down.
Where's your dad this time?'
   'Hospital,' puffed Billy.
'Tonsils out.'

'Bad luck!' said Springer.
'Tell him to rest his voice. Now,
let's sort this team out.'

'I'm glad you're here,' panted
Billy. 'We need you.'

'You certainly do need me,
boy,' barked Mr Bawl,
marching past. 'The trainer is
the most important member of
the team.'

'Who's he?' asked Springer.

'Mr Bawl,' gasped Billy.
'Dad sent him to coach us. He
can go now you're here.'

Springer frowned.

'Sorry, lad,' he said. 'PhIFA
rule number twenty-six – *A
ghost coach* – that's me – *may
not take the place of an official
coach* – that's him. *And if the*

ghost coach interferes he gets the sack – I disappear.'

Billy flopped down on the pitch.

'So we've got to put up with Mr Bawl!'

Mr Bawl marched them on to the pitch for a practice game. Billy kicked off to Kim. She passed nervously to Rob. He

tapped it feebly back to Billy.
Mr Bawl paced up and down
on the touchline watching them
like a hawk. Springer paced up
and down behind him.

'The Tigers are a good side,'
thought Billy. 'We'll show Mr
Bawl.'

He took the ball up the wing.
'Pass!' boomed Mr Bawl.

Billy dodged round Blocker.
Kim was making a run
alongside him.

'Pass back!' thundered Mr
Bawl.

But Billy and Kim had
practised their one-two a
thousand times. And this was
the moment for it. Billy passed
to Kim, wrong-footing Lisa.

Kim knocked it back to him.
Billy blasted the ball into the
back of the net. It was a great
goal.

'Well done, Tigers,' called
Springer.

'That was just luck,' shouted
Mr Bawl, his hands on his hips.
Springer copied him. There was
nothing to stop him making fun

of the official coach. He'd
checked in his PhIFA rule book.

'If I say "pass back" you
pass back,' bellowed Mr Bawl,
wagging his finger.

Springer wagged his finger
too.

'Don't forget,' yelled Mr
Bawl, 'the trainer is the most
important member of the team!'

Springer saluted. Billy
sniggered.

'Are you laughing, boy?'

'No, Mr Bawl,' said Billy,
pretending to cough.

Mr Bawl gave a blast on his
whistle. Bullseye was so nervous
he kicked off straight to the
opposition. Billy gave the ball a

wild kick. It hit Joe on the
elbow, bounced off Ellen's ear,
whacked Blocker on the back of
the head and trickled towards
Terry. Terry swung a tired foot
and fell on his bottom. Lisa

tried to take possession and tripped over Rick. Rob and Kim collided and Mona fell on top of them. It was a disaster.

'Call yourselves a good side?' bellowed Mr Bawl. 'My auntie's budgie plays better than you.'

'I bet his auntie's budgie is a better coach,' moaned Springer.

'There'll be a practice tomorrow before the match,' shouted Mr Bawl. 'Eleven o'clock sharp.'

He marched off.

'Can't you do anything?' Billy asked Springer.

'I know what I'm doing,' said Bullseye. 'I'm going home.'

'Not you, Bullseye,' sighed Billy.

'And I'm not coming back,' said Bullseye.

'You must,' said Billy. 'We're playing the Jets tomorrow. We always beat them.'

'Not with Mr Bawl, we won't,' moaned Lisa.

'We'll look really stupid,'
said Terry, crossly.

'You can't let your dad
down,' said Springer.

'We can't let Dad down,'
said Billy. 'He's already
worried about missing the
match.'

'I didn't miss any matches,'

said Blocker, 'when I had my tonsils out.'

'You weren't in the team then,' said Ellen. 'You were only three!'

'Never mind Blocker's tonsils,' sighed Billy. 'We'll have our own practice tomorrow. Come early. Agreed?'

The Tigers nodded. They slunk off home, their tails between their legs. Billy and Springer watched them go.

'Even my coaching's better than Mr Bawl's,' said Billy. 'But can't you give me some tips?'

'Sorry, lad,' said Springer.
'You're on your own. If I break
the rules, you'll never see me
again. Your dad has chosen Mr
Bawl for your official
coach . . .'

'That's it,' yelled Billy. 'I'll
get Dad to unchoose him.'

Billy and Springer arrived at
Tottingham Town hospital.
Dad was in the children's ward.
He was playing snap.

Springer dribbled round the
beds. Billy told Dad about Mr
Bawl.

'We don't need him,' said
Billy. 'Springer can . . . I mean
I can do the coaching. I've
done it before.'

GIVE HIM A CHANCE YOU'LL GET USED TO HIM. HE'S AN EXCELLENT COACH.

Dad got a pen and paper out of his pyjama pocket.

Your place is up front scoring goals, he wrote. *Not on the touchline.*

'But he's a terrible trainer,' said Springer.

'But he's a terrible trainer,

Dad,' said Billy.

Give him a chance, Dad wrote. *You'll get used to him. He's an excellent coach.*

'Who told him that?' asked Springer.

'Who told you that?' asked Billy.

Someone at work. Can't remember who. Come to think of it – it was Mr Bawl.

Springer threw his ball at Dad's head.

'But Dad!' wailed Billy.

Good luck on Saturday. Hope I can be there.

Dad went back to his game.

Billy arrived at the park nice and early next morning. The Tigers and Springer were standing in a row. They looked at Billy in despair. Mr Bawl was already there.

'What time do you call this?' he yelled at Billy. 'We're waiting for you. Look lively.Kit inspection.'

By the time the Jets turned

up, the Tigers had had enough.
But Mr Bawl hadn't.

'What are you going to do
when you get out there?' he
shouted.

'Play football?' quavered the
Tigers.

'You're going to win! What
are you going to do?'

'We're going to win,'
muttered the team.

'Not with your coaching,
they won't,' said Springer.

'The trainer is the most

important member of the
team,' said Mr Bawl. 'Who's
the most important member of
the team?'

'You are, Mr Bawl,'
mumbled the Tigers.

They walked glumly on to the
pitch. For the first time in their
lives, the Tigers didn't want to
play football. Mr Bawl strutted
along the touchline. Springer
strutted along behind him
pulling faces. The whistle blew.
The Jets kicked off. It wasn't
long before the Tigers were
two-nil down.

'You miserable worms!'
shouted Mr Bawl from the
touchline. 'I've seen better

footwork from my uncle's pet rattlesnake.'

'Every time I want to go forwards,' moaned Billy to the others, 'he calls me back.'

'I could've got the ball off that striker,' said Terry, 'if he hadn't shouted at me.'

'He told me to pass,' said
Blocker, 'and I didn't even have
the ball.'

'I wish he'd tell me to go
home,' said Bullseye.

'If only Dad was here,'
thought Billy. 'He'd see how
bad Mr Bawl is.'

The Tigers were giving up.
Even Springer wasn't watching
any more.

But suddenly Springer leapt
in the air. He waved wildly at
Billy. He ran along the
touchline.

'Billy!' he yelled. 'Come
here.'

Billy slouched over.

'Where do you think you're going?' shouted Mr Bawl.

'What do you want?' Billy asked Springer.

'I want you to get back into position,' yelled Mr Bawl.

At that moment, the ball came Billy's way.

49

'Take possession, Billy,' called Springer. 'Go on. There's space down the wing.'

'But Springer,' said Billy. 'You mustn't coach us! Remember?'

But Springer carried on.

'Look out for that defender. Screen the ball.'

As if in a dream, Billy did.
He could see the chance to
score. But what was going to
happen to Springer?

'Don't hog the ball, boy,'
shouted Mr Bawl, as Billy
passed the last defender. 'Pull
back!'

'Carry on,' called Springer.
'The goalie's off his line.
Steady. Chip it over his head
. . . and . . . it's a goal!'

The Tigers rushed over to
Billy.

But Billy wasn't excited. He
couldn't see Springer anywhere.
Springer had risked everything
to help them score a goal and
now he had disappeared. Billy
would never see him again.

Head down, he turned to walk back to the centre.

'We're a great team, Billy,' called a voice.

It was Springer, doing chin-ups on the goalpost!

'You're still here!' shouted Billy.

'Of course we're still here,' said Joe.

'I wanted to go home,' said Bullseye. 'Till you scored that goal.'

'Get to your positions!' yelled Mr Bawl.

'You don't have to listen to him any more,' said Springer.

'What do you mean?' asked Billy.

'He's not a proper coach. I've

found out all about him. I was
listening to Lisa's grandad. He
told Blocker's mum that
Tottingham Town Council told
Mr Bawl he was banned
because he's so bad.'

'So you can coach us and
you won't disappear!'

Billy had to tell the team
quickly.

'Mr Bawl's not a proper coach,' he whispered to Bullseye. 'Don't listen to him. I'll do the coaching. Pass it on.'

The Jets kicked off. Blocker won possession and passed to Ellen. But she was surrounded by defenders. There was no way forwards.

'Pass back to Blocker,' called Springer.

'Forwards run!' shouted Mr Bawl.

Billy panicked.

'Pass Blocker back and run!' he yelled.

The Tigers stopped in their tracks and stared at him.

'Keep quiet, boy!' yelled Mr Bawl. 'I'm the trainer.'

The ball went out of play. Blocker went to take the throw.

'To Joe,' shouted Springer. 'He's unmarked.'

'Don't throw it up the field!' yelled Mr Bawl.

'Throw Joe up the field,' called Billy.

Blocker didn't know what to

do. He lobbed the ball wildly
with all his strength just as Mr
Bawl strode up to Billy.

'I'm sending you off, boy,' he
snarled.

Just then Blocker's throw
came zooming towards him. It
hit him on the back of the
head. Mr Bawl fell flat on his

face. He was out cold. Blocker's
mum pulled him to the
touchline.

Now the Tigers could play
their natural game. Terry got
possession after kick-off and
sent a lofted pass up to
Bullseye.

'Rob's unmarked!' yelled Springer.

'To Rob!' shouted Billy.

Rob took the ball on his chest and chipped it to Kim. Her diving header found the back of the net. Two-all. Springer jumped up and down with excitement.

The Tigers rushed back for the kick-off. Someone arrived at the edge of the pitch. He held up a big piece of paper. It was Billy's dad.

They let me out early.

'Great!' yelled Billy.

The Tigers cheered.

Where's Mr Bawl?

'He's on the touchline,' laughed Billy.

The match was nearly over.
The Jets made a final desperate
push forwards. A striker took a
wild shot but it deflected off
Blocker. It was going to be an
own goal. Then Mona the

goalkeeper dived for the ball. She gathered it safely into her chest. It was a brilliant save. And her goal kick was even better. It dropped right at Billy's feet. He swerved round one defender. But there was another coming up fast. Kim was running alongside him.

'One-two,' shouted Springer.

Billy passed to Kim. The defender followed the ball, leaving Billy unmarked. Kim passed the ball back to him. He tamed her volley on the inside of his foot and slammed it into the back of the net. It was three-two. The final whistle blew. The Tigers had won the match.